For Luise and Natascha

This edition first published in 2019 by Gecko Press
PO Box 9335, Wellington 6141, New Zealand
info@geckopress.com

Text and illustrations: Jörg Mühle
Title of the original edition: *Zwei für mich, einer für dich*
© 2018 Moritz Verlag, Frankfurt am Main
English-language edition arranged through Mundt Agency, Düsseldorf

Edited by Penelope Todd
Typesetting by Katrina Duncan
Printed in China by Everbest Printing Co. Ltd,
an accredited ISO 14001 & FSC-certified printer

ISBN hardback: 978-1-776572-39-7
ISBN paperback: 978-1-776572-40-3

For more curiously good books, visit geckopress.com

Jörg Mühle

Two For Me,
One For You

GECKO PRESS

On her way home, Bear found three mushrooms.

Weasel was very excited. He wiped the mushrooms, seared them, seasoned them with plenty of salt and pepper, and let them simmer in the frying pan with a little parsley.

Bear dished up. "One mushroom for you
and one mushroom for me," she said.
"And another mushroom for me. That's fair.
I'm big, so I need to eat a lot."

Weasel did not agree. "One mushroom for me,
one mushroom for you, and another one for me.
That's fair! I'm small, and I still have to grow."

"One for you, two for me. That's fair, because I found the mushrooms."

"That's not fair at all! You brought them home to me! And I did all the work. I wiped the mushrooms and seared them and seasoned them and simmered them in the heavy pan. With parsley!"

"But you used my recipe! And I set the table. And anyway, I like mushrooms much more than you do," said Bear.

"Mushrooms are my absolute all-time number-one food! And I'm so hungry. You can hear my stomach grumbling."

"Wait! I'm much bigger than you, so my hunger is bigger! My stomach's been grumbling so long it's gone croaky."

"But I said first that
my stomach's grumbling!"

"But I said I wanted the extra mushroom first!"

"One mushroom less won't hurt you!"

"Too many mushrooms aren't good for little weasels!"

"Or for fat bears."

"Okay, that does it!
Two for me, one for you,
and that's it!"

"In that case, you're not my friend any more."

Bear and Weasel were stunned.
"The cheek of it!" they shouted.
"Totally unfair! Can you believe it?"

"He just swiped our mushroom!"

But then they wished each other bon appetit.
The mushrooms tasted wonderful.

There was even dessert.

"Wild strawberries!" cried Bear, delighted.
"My absolute all-time number-one food!"

Weasel dished them up...